Be a Ballerina!

Inspired by the teleplay "Dance to the Rescue,"
by Eric Weiner

Illustrated by Warner McGee

A GOLDEN BOOK · NEW YORK

ISBN: 978-0-375-85749-2
www.randomhouse.com/kids
MANUFACTURED IN CHINA

¡Hola! I'm Dora. Do you like to dance?

I love to dress up and dance!

I like to do country-western dancing.

Decorate these boots
for some fancy cowboy dancing!

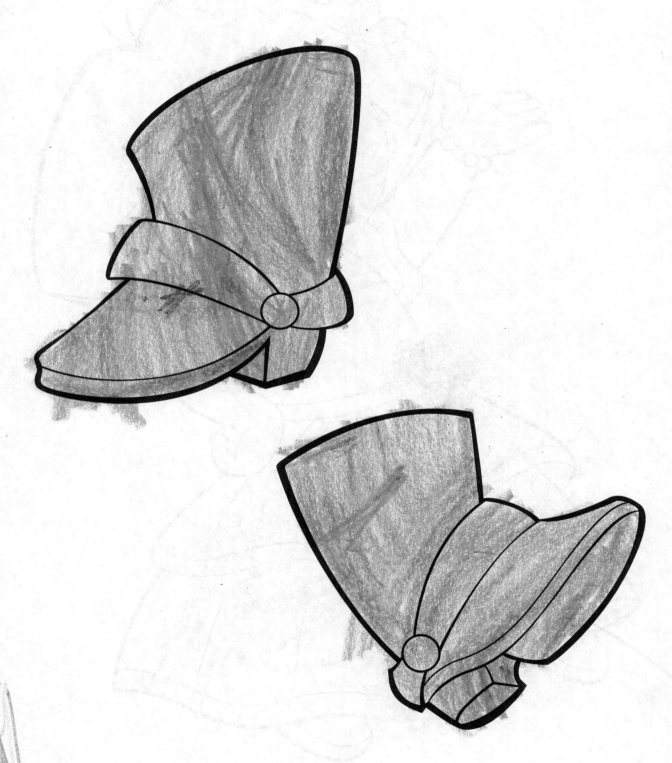

Sometimes I do a Spanish dance called flamenco!

Sometimes Boots and I dance together.

Will you circle the picture that is different?

A

B

C

D

Boots is a great dancer.

Boots is so graceful!

Boots can even tap-dance!

Boots's favorite dance is the Silly Monkey Dance.

Draw yourself doing the Silly Monkey Dance with me.

Draw a line connecting the dance moves on the left to the matching shapes on the right.

Abuela says it's time to go to dance practice—
and after that is the big recital!

Let's go to the dancing school, Boots!

Trace the path that will take us to the bridge.

Oh, no! The marching ants won't let us pass . . .
unless we dance like ants!

Help us stay on the path by following the numbers from 1 to 10.

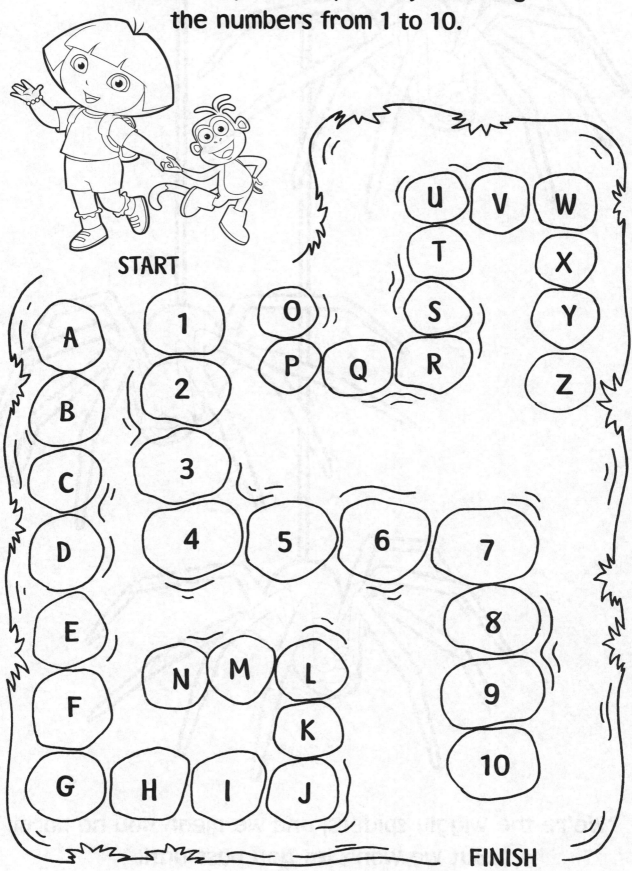

START

FINISH

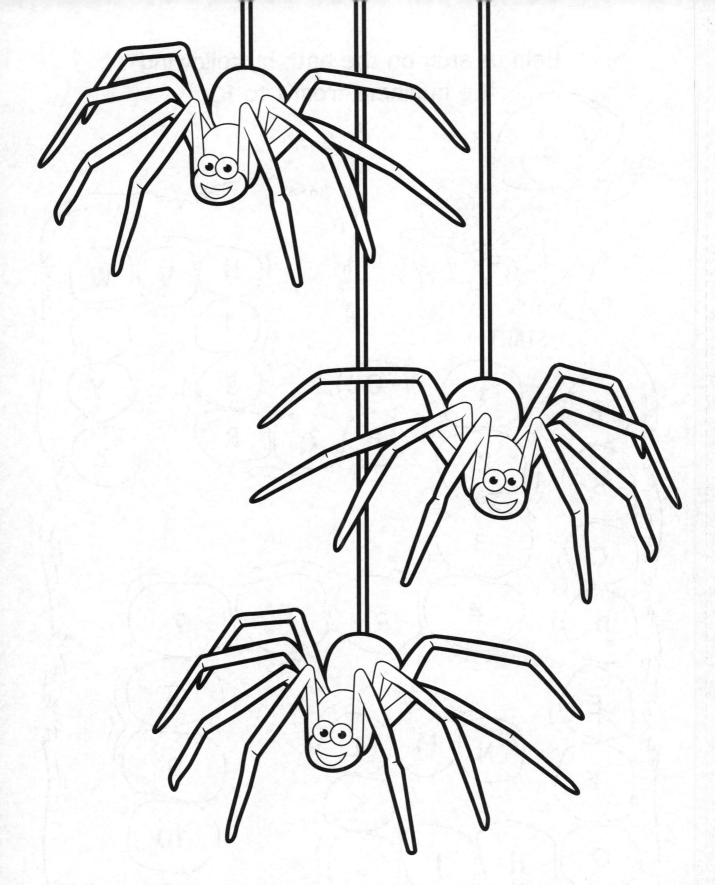

"We're the wiggly spiders, and we mean you no harm.
But we won't let you pass until
you wiggle your arms."

Let's wiggle our arms and wiggle our wrists!
Wiggle, wiggle, wiggle like this!

"That was fun, Dora.
I can't wait to get to the dancing school."

Those sneaky snakes won't let us by . . . unless we slide like them from side to side.

Put your hands together, then slither and slide!

That was great marching, wiggling, and sliding!
Thank you for your help!

Follow the path marked DANCE
to help Dora get to school.

D R E S S S

D A N C E

D O L L S

SCHOOL

Use the key to help Boots get ready for practice.

KEY			
1 = Purple	2 = Yellow	3 = Red	4 = Blue

Look at this page. Then look at the next one.
How many differences can you find?

ANSWER: On this page, the gym bag is missing; Swiper is now in the room; there is another shoe; and there is a soccer ball.

I wear a leotard at dance practice.

I'm practicing my ballet for the big recital.

Circle the shoes Dora should wear to dance ballet.

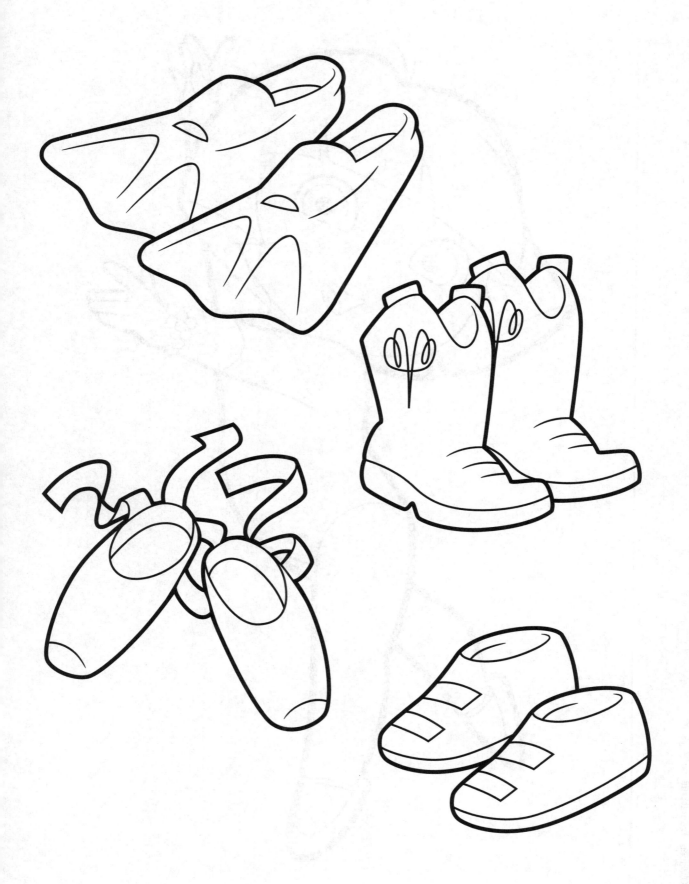

Oh, no! Here comes that sneaky fox, Swiper!

Swiper is trying to swipe my ballet shoes!
Swiper, no swiping!

"I'm sorry. I like swiping,
but I really like dancing, too."

Since Swiper likes dancing,
he should be in the recital with us!

"Thank you, Dora! That would be great!"

Circle the Swiper that is different.

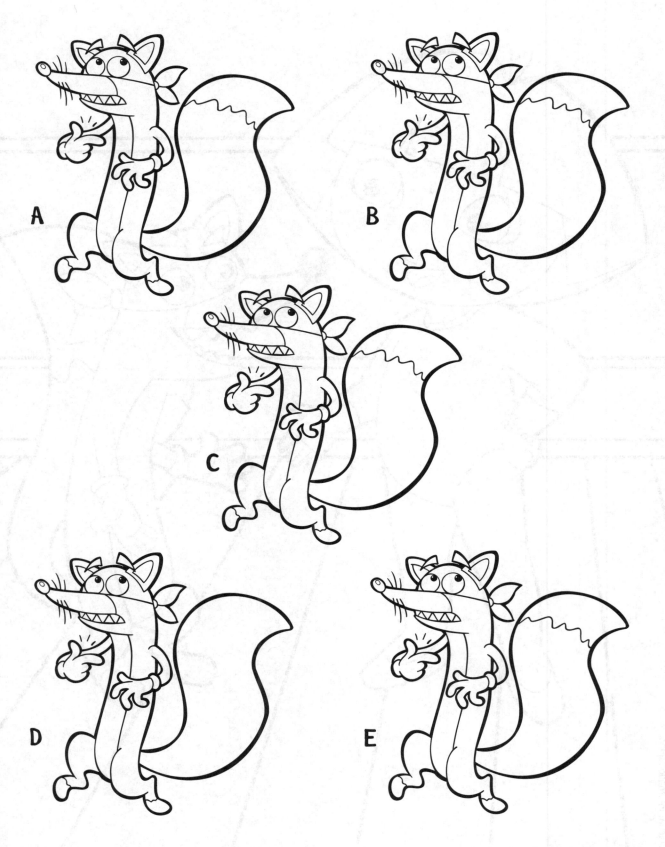

Draw a line connecting the dance moves on the left to the matching shapes on the right.

Look! Our families are here to watch the recital.

Boots can't wait to dance!

Boots wants to look special for the big recital.
Trace and color a fancy bow tie for him.

Ballerinas wear tutus.
Add some shiny stickers to mine to make it sparkly.

Come on! Let's dance! *¡Vamos a bailar!*

Everyone can dance!

Tico is doing the Ants in His Pants Dance.

Boogie, Benny. Boogie!

Wow, Boots and Isa are wonderful dance partners!

The big finish!

Look at Swiper go!

"All together now!"

Make up your own dance,
then draw you and your best
friend doing it.

"Bravo, Dora!"

Draw a line to connect the pose on the left to the matching pose on the right.

"Dora is a beautiful ballerina!"

Mami and Papi are so proud of me!

Take a bow, everyone!

Use the key to color these flowers for Dora.

KEY
1 = Green   2 = Yellow   3 = Red   4 = Blue

Thank you, Boots. They're beautiful!

Thank you for all your help.
I really loved dancing with you.